This book belongs to:

....

D0256086

Note to parents and carers

Read it yourself is a series of classic, traditional tales, written in a simple way to give children a confident and successful start to reading.

Each book is carefully structured to include many high-frequency words that are vital for first reading. The sentences on each page are supported closely by pictures to help with reading, and to offer lively details to talk about.

The books are graded into four levels that progressively introduce wider vocabulary and longer stories as a reader's ability grows.

Ideas for use

- Ask how your child would like to approach reading at this stage. Would he prefer to hear you read the story first, or would he like to read the story to you and see how he gets on?

- Help him to sound out any words he does not know.

- Developing readers can be concentrating so hard on the words that they sometimes don't fully grasp the meaning of what they're reading. Answering the puzzle questions on pages 46 and 47 will help with understanding.

For more information and advice, visit www.ladybird.com/readityourself

Level 3 is ideal for children who are developing reading confidence and stamina, and who are eager to read longer stories with a wider vocabulary.

Special features:

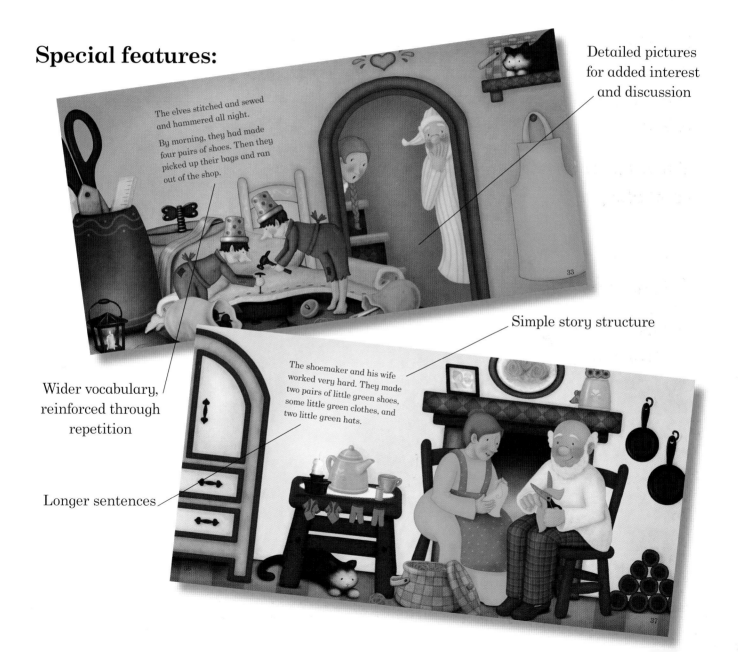

Detailed pictures for added interest and discussion

The elves stitched and sewed and hammered all night.

By morning, they had made four pairs of shoes. Then they picked up their bags and ran out of the shop.

Simple story structure

The shoemaker and his wife worked very hard. They made two pairs of little green shoes, some little green clothes, and two little green hats.

Wider vocabulary, reinforced through repetition

Longer sentences

Educational Consultant: Geraldine Taylor

A catalogue record for this book is available from the British Library

Published by Ladybird Books Ltd
80 Strand, London, WC2R 0RL
A Penguin Company

2 4 6 8 10 9 7 5 3 1
© LADYBIRD BOOKS LTD MMX
Ladybird, Read It Yourself and the Ladybird Logo are registered or
unregistered trade marks of Ladybird Books Limited.

ISBN: 978-1-40930-359-6

Printed in China

The Elves and the Shoemaker

Illustrated by Virginia Allyn

Once upon a time, there was a poor shoemaker and his wife.

"This is all the leather I have left," said the poor shoemaker. "I can make just one pair of shoes."

That night, the shoemaker cut the leather.

"I'll make these shoes in the morning," he said. He left the leather in the shop and went to bed.

9

The next morning, the shoemaker came downstairs. To his surprise, the leather had been made into a pair of beautiful shoes.

The shoemaker called his wife.
"Did you make these shoes?"

"No," said his wife, "I didn't
make those shoes!"

Just then, a rich lady came into the shop. She picked up the shoes.

"These are the most beautiful shoes I have ever seen," she said.

She gave the shoemaker three gold coins.

With the money, the shoemaker bought some more leather.

That night, the shoemaker cut out two pairs of shoes. He left the leather on the table and went to bed.

17

In the morning, there were two pairs of shoes on the table.

The shoemaker called his wife.

"Did you make these shoes?"

"No," said his wife. "I didn't make those shoes!"

That very morning, a rich man came into the shop.

"What beautiful shoes," said the man. "I must have them. I will pay you six gold coins."

The shoemaker bought some more leather.

"Now I can make three pairs of shoes," he said.

He worked late into the night cutting the leather. Then he went to bed.

The next morning, the shoemaker came downstairs.

On the table were three pairs of beautiful shoes.

25

The shoemaker called his wife.

"We must find out who is making these beautiful shoes for us," said the shoemaker.

The next night, the shoemaker worked very hard. He cut the leather for four pairs of shoes. But this time, the shoemaker and his wife hid in the shop.

At midnight, the door of the
shop opened and in came
two little elves dressed in
rags. They jumped up onto
the table and opened their
little green bags.

The elves stitched and sewed
and hammered all night.

By morning, they had made
four pairs of shoes. Then they
picked up their bags and ran
out of the shop.

The shoemaker said to his wife, "The elves have helped us, but how can we help them?"

"I know what we can do!" said his wife.

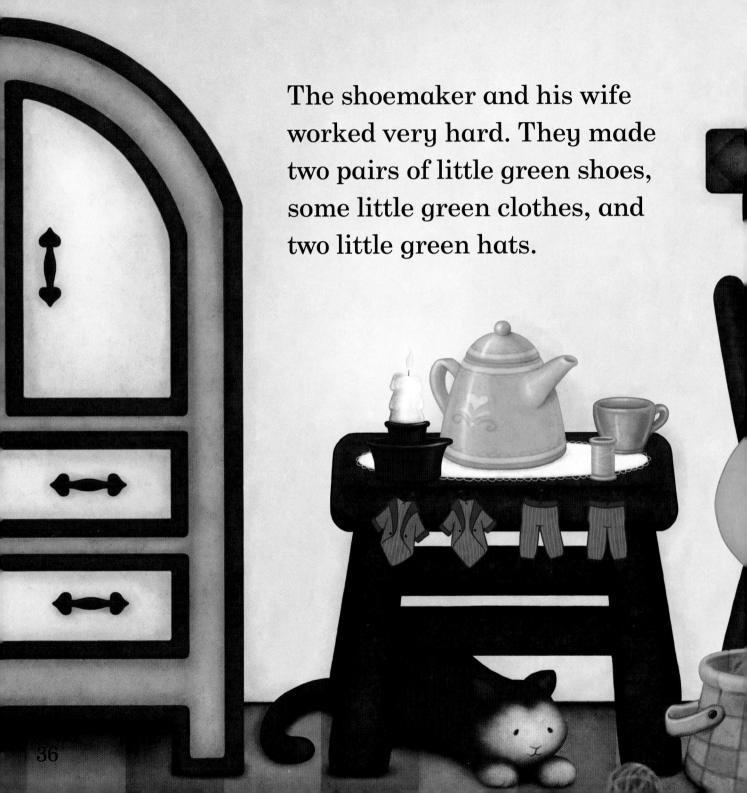

The shoemaker and his wife worked very hard. They made two pairs of little green shoes, some little green clothes, and two little green hats.

That night, they left the little green shoes, hats and clothes in the shop. Then they hid again.

At midnight, the door of the shop opened and the elves came in.

When they saw the little green shoes, the little green clothes and the little green hats, they were very surprised. They put them on at once.

The little elves went on helping the shoemaker and his wife to make beautiful shoes. And the shoemaker and his wife made more clothes for the little elves.

42

And the shoemaker and his wife, and the two little elves all lived happily ever after.

How much do you remember about the story of The Elves and the Shoemaker? Answer these questions and find out!

- How much money does the rich lady pay for the beautiful shoes?

- How much money does the rich man pay for the shoes?

- What time do the elves come into the shop?

- What material does the shoemaker buy to make the shoes?

- What does the shoemaker's wife make for the elves?

Look at the different story sentences and match them to the people who said them.

"This is all the leather I have left."

"These are the most beautiful shoes I have ever seen."

"No, I didn't make those shoes!"

"I will pay you six gold coins."

Read it yourself
with Ladybird

The Three Billy Goats Gruff — Level 1

Cinderella — Level 1

Little Red Hen — Level 1

Goldilocks and the Three Bears — Level 1

The Magic Porridge Pot — Level 1

The Ugly Duckling — Level 1

The Gingerbread Man — Level 2

Sleeping Beauty — Level 2

Sly Fox and Red Hen — Level 2

The Three Little Pigs — Level 2

Town Mouse and Country Mouse — Level 2

Little Red Riding Hood — Level 2

The Elves and the Shoemaker — Level 3

Jack and the Beanstalk — Level 3

The Pied Piper of Hamelin — Level 4

The Wizard of Oz — Level 4

Collect all the titles in the series.